D0601479

Withdrawn from Stock
Dublin City Public Libraries

This book
belongs to

.....................................

# Cuddle
## The Magic Kitten

## SUPERSTAR DREAMS

# Cuddle
## The Magic Kitten

Leabharlanna Poiblí Chathair Baile Átha Cliath

Dublin City Public Libraries

## SUPERSTAR DREAMS
by Hayley Daze

Willow
Tree

A CIP catalogue record for this book is
available from the British Library

This edition published by Willow Tree Books, 2018
Willow Tree Books, Tide Mill Way, Woodbridge, Suffolk, IP12 1AP
First published by Ladybird Books Ltd.

0 2 4 6 8 9 7 5 3 1

Series created by Working Partners Limited,
London, WC1X 9HH
Text © 2018 Working Partners
Cover illustration © 2018 Willow Tree Books
Interior illustrations © 2018 Willow Tree Books

Special thanks to Elizabeth Galloway

Willow Tree Books and associated logos are trademarks and/or
registered trademarks of Tide Mill Media Ltd

ISBN: 978-1-78700-447-4
Printed and bound in Great Britain
by Bell and Bain Ltd, Glasgow

www.willowtreebooks.net

For James and Victoria – good times

Cuddle the kitten has black-and-white fur,
A cute crooked tail, and a very loud purr.
Her two best friends, Olivia and Grace,
Know Cuddle's world is a special place!

Just give her a cuddle, then everything spins;
A twitch of her whiskers, and magic begins!
So if you see a sunbeam, and hear Cuddle's bell,
You can join in the adventures as well!

# Contents

# Chapter One
## Treetop Tumble

A breeze rippled through the cherry
tree, making its pink blossom dance.
Grace's combat trousers and T-shirt
were scattered with sweet-smelling
petals.

"It's like being in a snowstorm
of petals," she called down to Olivia.

PEMBROKE BRANCH TEL. 6689575

"Climb up and see."

"I've never climbed a tree before," Olivia said, twirling one of her curls round and round a finger.

The girls were in Olivia's back

garden. Grace was sitting in the cherry tree, while Olivia stood beside the trunk.

From her perch, Grace could see her own back garden next door. The roofs of the houses that lined their street were still damp from a rain shower. The sky over Catterton was dark grey.

"Let's see if you can get up here before it rains again," Grace said. "I'll help you."

"All right," Olivia said. "Here goes." Stretching up on to the tips of her shoes, she grabbed the lowest branch.

"That's it," Grace said. "Now wrap your legs round the trunk and hold the next branch."

Olivia could see Grace's smiling face through the leaves, framed by her blonde hair. She stretched up for the branch, but her fingers slid over a patch of moss. With a shriek, she tumbled to the ground.

Grace scrambled down after her. "Are you OK?"

Olivia was lying on the ground, her black curls fanned out like a halo. "I'm fine," she said, smiling. "Now do you believe I can't climb trees?"

Grace pulled Olivia to her feet. "You just need to practise. Then you'll be able to climb like a cat!"

Just then, a sunbeam pushed its way through the clouds, scattering golden rays.

Olivia clapped her hands. "Oh! Do you think Cuddle's on her way?"

Cuddle was a cute kitten who had appeared in a beam of sunlight and taken the girls on a magical adventure.

*Jingle jangle jingle.*

"That's Cuddle's bell!" Grace cried.

The sunbeam shone on Olivia's bike, which was propped up against the back of the house. A pink basket was fixed to the handlebars. It wiggled and jiggled, and Cuddle's cute little face poked out. Her blue eyes sparkled in the sun.

"Hello, Cuddle!" both girls cried.

Olivia grinned. "The sunbeam looks like a spotlight. Cuddle's a movie star."

# Cuddle
### The Magic Kitten

The kitten's bell jingled as she sprang on to the edge of the bike's basket. With a swish of her tail, she leapt into Grace's arms and greeted her friends with a happy "Miaow!"

Grace hugged the kitten tightly. "You certainly live up to your name, don't you, Cuddle?" she said.

*Purrrrrrrrr*, went Cuddle. She sounded like a tiny rumble of thunder.

The girls' skin tingled as if Cuddle's whiskers were tickling them. Cuddle's purr grew louder and louder, and the girls started to giggle. They leaned towards each other, the little kitten cradled between them.

Now they knew what would happen next – kitten magic! They each shut their eyes and the garden and the cherry tree faded away ...

***

Grace's eyes fluttered open. She was lying on a hard surface in the pitch dark. She closed her eyes and tried opening them again, but it was no good. She couldn't see a thing.

"Olivia?" Grace asked. She could feel her heart thumping.

"I'm here," said Olivia. The two girls were lying side by side.

Olivia knew that Grace was afraid of the dark, and squeezed her friend's hand. "*Where are we?*" she wondered.

# Cuddle
### The Magic Kitten

Grace reached inside the pocket of her combat trousers. Her shaking fingers closed over her torch and she flicked it on. A narrow beam of light

shone out, and the girls could see that they were surrounded by walls.

Grace rapped the wall above them with her knuckles. It gave a hollow echo.

"That sounds like wood," she said. "I think we're inside some kind of box."

Olivia gulped. "We're trapped!"

# Cuddle
### The Magic Kitten

# Chapter Two
## In the Spotlight

"Miaow!" went Cuddle, from somewhere by their feet. Grace shone the torch at the kitten as she skipped up between them, her fur tickling their bare arms. She rubbed against Olivia's neck, then touched Grace's nose with her own.

"It's like she's telling us not to be scared," Grace said. She tried to stroke Cuddle's ears, but the kitten ducked out of the beam of light and Grace's fingers found the bend in her tail instead.

The girls jumped as a booming voice echoed over them. "Ladies and gentlemen! I'm glad you're all sitting down, as this next trick would have you falling over in amazement."

There was a distant ripple of laughter.

"Who's that?" Olivia whispered to Grace.

The voice continued. "May I present the Magic Box of Doom!"

"The Magic Box of Doom," Grace repeated. "Do you think that's where we are?" Her voice trembled.

*Slam!* A tiny door opened in the wall behind the girls' heads, letting in a stream of light. *Slam! Slam!*

Two more doors opened by their feet. *Slam! Slam!* A door opened on Olivia's side of the box, then another on Grace's.

The sudden brightness made the girls blink. Grace switched off her torch and put it back in her pocket.

Cuddle walked up to the opening behind their heads and sniffed it.

"Good idea, Cuddle," Olivia said. "Let's find out where we are."

She wriggled head first towards the opening, arching her back like a caterpillar. Grace shifted out of her way, using her elbows to move towards the bottom of the box.

"I can fit my legs through those

two holes," Grace said. She stuck them through, waving her trainers around.

Olivia grabbed the rim of the tiny doorway. She pulled herself up so her head poked through the opening – and gave a gasp of amazement.

The box seemed to be mounted on a stand. It was painted blue, with a golden latch shaped like a lion's paw fixed just above the opening. Clusters of spotlights hung from the ceiling above Olivia, behind a red velvet curtain that had been drawn up. To one side was a bank of seats, filled with rows of people. They were whispering to each other and pointing at her.

A grin spread over Olivia's face.

"Grace, we're onstage!" She stuck her
hand through one of the side openings
and waved at the audience. "This is
brilliant. I've always wanted to be
an actress."

A boy a little older than Olivia and Grace was standing at the back of the stage. He was wearing a blue suit and he had a gold sash around his waist. His top hat was too big for him and flopped down over one ear. He was staring at Olivia, his eyes wide with surprise. She realised he must be the owner of the booming voice.

The boy gave himself a shake, making his top hat fall over the other ear. "Looks like I've already got an assistant," he said.

He drew out a long, shiny sword from his sash.

The audience gasped.

*What's he going to do?*

thought Olivia.

"Ladies and gentlemen," the boy
said, "I will now cut this girl in half!"

# Cuddle
## The Magic Kitten

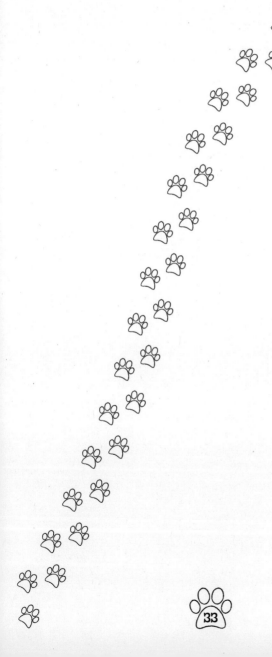

# Chapter Three
## Cuddle the Conjuring Kitten

"Oh no," Grace called from inside the box. "Please don't chop us in two!"

The boy's eyebrows shot up so high they disappeared under the brim of his hat. To him, it must have sounded as if Olivia's tummy was talking.

He gripped the sword's handle

tightly and raised it above his head. Olivia noticed that he was red in the face as he spoke to the audience. "Now I've got my sword, we can get to the *point* of the trick."

The audience laughed. From somewhere offstage came a rattling drum roll.

Inside the box, Cuddle's ears twitched and Grace saw the kitten's blue eyes flash. Cuddle scampered along Grace's legs and pushed her furry body through one of the holes at Grace's feet. Then she perched on the toe of one of her trainers.

The audience exclaimed in delight.

"Look at that kitten," Olivia heard an

old lady say. "How cute!"

The boy shook his head as he tried to work out where Cuddle had come from. The top hat flopped down over both his ears. "Ladies and gentlemen," he said, "a big hand – I mean a big paw! – for …"

"Her name's Cuddle," Olivia whispered.

"A big paw for Cuddle the Conjuring Kitten!" he finished.

The audience clapped and cheered.

"Now," the boy said, "are you ready to be amazed by the Magic Box of Doom?"

"Yes!" the audience shouted.

Olivia held her breath. She felt

Grace's hand wrap round one of her ankles. He wasn't really going to cut them in two, was he? *It's just a magic trick*, Olivia tried to convince herself.

The boy swung his sword towards the box. As it sliced through the air, Cuddle pounced on the lion's-paw latch. *Click!* The latch sprang open and the box fell apart, the walls and lid crashing to the ground. Out tumbled Olivia and Grace. Cuddle jumped clear, landing beside them.

The boy dropped his sword in shock.

Olivia looked up at him. "We're sorry Cuddle ruined your magic trick," she said.

# Cuddle
### The Magic Kitten

"She didn't ruin it," the boy replied. "She made it even better!"

He pulled Olivia and Grace to their feet, and turned to the audience. "It turns out I'm an even better magician than I realised. Instead of cutting a girl in half, I've doubled her!"

"I think that makes you a mathematician rather than a magician," Grace said with a grin.

The audience got to its feet, cheering and whistling. The boy raised his arm above his head and swept down in a bow, making his top hat fall off. Grace bowed too, and Olivia dropped into a deep curtsy. Cuddle jumped inside the top hat, just her little whiskered face poking out.

Olivia nudged Grace. "I told you Cuddle was a star!"

# Chapter Four
## Good Luck Charm

Grace squinted past the glare of the spotlights. At the front of the audience was a table with three people sitting behind it. A large silver sign was fixed to the table, with 'Star Maker' written across it in swirly red letters.

"We're at a talent show," she said.

"They must be the judges."

Cuddle sprang off the stage, landing on the judges' table.

TONY      ELISSA      NICK

STAR Maker

Two of the judges, a woman in a purple dress and a man in a red jacket, stroked the little kitten. She rolled over in front of the third judge, a man with gelled hair and a tight white T-shirt, knocking over his nameplate. It said 'Tony'.

"Nice to meet you, Cuddle the Conjuring Kitten," Tony said, tickling her tummy. He looked up at the boy onstage.

"You've definitely got star potential," Tony said to the boy. "And so has Cuddle," he added, with a wink at the kitten.

As the curtain came down, the boy cried, "Thank you, Cuddle – you made my act *purr*-fect!"

Cuddle raced offstage, with Grace and Olivia right behind her, and darted through a half-open door.

"I wonder why she's taking us here," Olivia said, spotting a sign that said 'Dressing Rooms'.

Grace pushed open the door and stared in wide-eyed amazement.

There were jugglers juggling, clowns laughing, gymnasts tumbling, dancers twirling, singers humming and even some performing animals.

Cuddle bounced up to a girl, who looked like she had stepped out of a history book, and leapt into her arms.

"Oh!" the girl exclaimed.

"Sorry. That's Cuddle and she's very friendly," Grace said.

The girl's face was as white as Cuddle's tummy. "Are you all right?" Olivia asked.

A woman was standing next to the girl, holding a book called *Poems by William Shakespeare*. She said, "Chloe's just nervous about performing her act. Aren't you, dear?"

Chloe nodded. She was trembling all over, from her red hair, which was pinned up in a bun, to her long emerald

dress, right the way down to her green shoes. Even her puffed sleeves were shaking.

"I'll be all right as long as I have my lucky charm," Chloe said. She held out her hand to show the girls a chain with a sparkling white jewel hanging from it. Cuddle batted it and watched it swing.

"It's beautiful," Olivia said.

"What's your

talent?" Grace asked.

"Chloe's dressed as a girl from Shakespeare's time," Chloe's mum said. "She's reciting one of his poems for her act."

A man burst through the door behind them, holding a clipboard. He wore a badge saying 'Stage Manager'. "Is Hypno the Great here?" he asked. "It's his turn to perform."

Another man, dressed in long blue robes with an orange turban on his head, weaved his way through the sea of performers.

"There you are," the stage manager said. "You'll be Hypno the Late if you don't hurry."

Hypno whirled round. "I need to find my crystal first. I think a monkey took it. It's essential to my act." His eyes lit up as he saw the necklace sparkling in Chloe's hand. "That's perfect! Can I borrow it?"

Before Chloe could reply, Hypno grabbed the necklace from her and ran out to the stage.

"My lucky necklace!" Chloe cried. "I can't perform without it." Her eyes welled with tears.

"I'll get it back," Grace said. "Hypno, wait!"

She sprinted after him, her legs pounding as if she was aiming for the finishing line at Sports Day.

Without thinking, Grace ran across the stage towards him, but there was a creak of rope and a *whoosh!* of velvet. The stage curtain was going up!

# Cuddle
## The Magic Kitten

# Chapter Five
# Cuddle Lends a Paw

Olivia, Cuddle, Chloe and her mum
watched from the wings of the stage
as Hypno gestured for Grace to sit in a
velvet chair. He sat down opposite her.

Chloe's mum had her arms folded
crossly as she spoke to the stage
manager. "I want my daughter's

necklace back now!"

"Keep the noise down, please," he replied. "Hypno's about to begin."

"Don't worry," Olivia said quietly to Chloe. "We'll get your necklace back as soon as he's finished his act – whatever it is."

"Hypnosis," the stage manager whispered. "That's what his name's short for. He puts people in a very deep sleep."

"What if Grace isn't sleepy?" Olivia asked.

"It doesn't matter," the stage manager said. "He'll make her sleep and tell her to do funny things."

Olivia gulped. Would Grace be

all right?

Onstage, Hypno held up Chloe's necklace between Grace's face and his own. He swung it gently.

"Keep your eyes fixed on the necklace," he said. "You'll soon be feeling tired."

Cuddle pushed between Olivia and Chloe and strolled on to the stage. She stood behind Hypno's chair, blinking in the spotlights.

"Cuddle!" Olivia whispered. "Come back!"

But the little kitten clambered up the back of Grace's chair. Her crooked tail twitched in time with the necklace as it swung back and forth.

"You're getting sleepy," Hypno told Grace. "Very sleepy ..."

But his own voice began to sound tired as his head swayed, following the movement of the necklace.

Grace watched Cuddle. The kitten swished her tail back and forth, faster

and faster, and the necklace became a
gleaming blur. Grace's eyes widened.
Cuddle was controlling it!

Hypno gave an enormous snore. He
tipped forward from his chair on to the
stage, where he curled up – fast asleep.

Grace giggled. "Cuddle made Hypno hypnotise himself!"

The stage manager ran onstage, his face red. "Er, ladies and gentlemen! We seem to – um – have a problem."

The necklace was still in Hypno's hand. Before Grace could reach it, two men with Star Maker T-shirts hurried past her. They each took one of Hypno's arms and dragged him away.

"Stop!" yelled Chloe's mum, running after them. "That's my daughter's lucky necklace!"

The stage manager rubbed his eyes. "Bring the curtain down, before anything else goes wrong!"

# Cuddle
## The Magic Kitten

As the curtain swished shut, Grace picked up Cuddle and joined Olivia and Chloe backstage.

"You need to get ready, Chloe," the stage manager called over, glancing at his clipboard. "It's nearly your turn to go onstage."

Chloe shook her head so hard that her bun started to tumble down. "Not without my necklace or my mum. I can't do it." Then she ran off.

Grace drew Olivia to one side. "I know why Cuddle's brought us here," Grace whispered. "We've got to help Chloe perform – whether she has her lucky necklace or not."

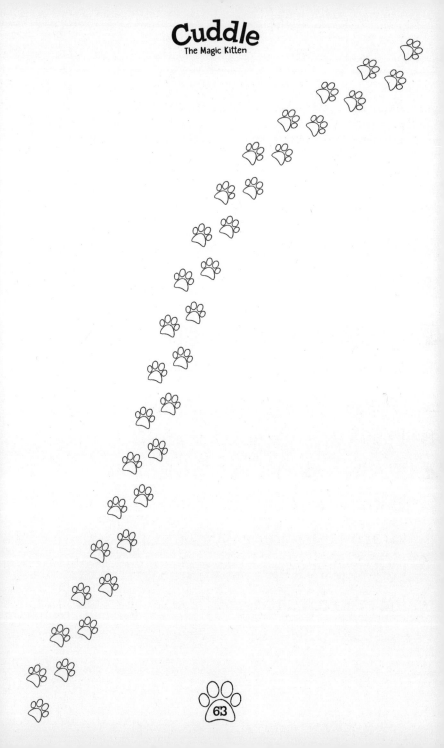

# Cuddle
### The Magic Kitten

# Chapter Six
## Chloe's Dream

Olivia, Grace and Cuddle raced after Chloe, but she was fast and they couldn't keep up. They ended up in a central hallway with lots of small practice rooms leading off from it – but there was no sign of Chloe.

Grace whirled around. "Where could

she have gone?"

Olivia looked inside one of the rooms. A group of boys wearing rollerblades and tracksuits were practising, mixing skating moves with breakdance spins and flips. Chloe wasn't there. Grace ran into

the next room. A troupe of dancers in multicoloured leotards and footless tights were doing leaps and twirls.

"Have you seen a girl in a green dress?" Grace asked. They shook their heads.

Cuddle jumped out of Grace's arms and trotted across the hallway. One of the doors was open a crack. She pushed her head through and it swung open. Grace and Olivia followed her inside.

A girl with pink hair was holding an electric guitar. "One, two, three!" she

cried and started playing, along with a girl on a keyboard and a boy on drums. 'The Krazy Katz' was painted on the largest drum. A crowd of other performers was watching The Krazy Katz practise. Cuddle gave a loud miaow, and jumped into the lap of a girl sitting cross-legged by the wall. It was Chloe!

Grace and Olivia glanced at each other. Chloe's eyes were red from crying. They went to sit either side of her, while Chloe ran her fingers through Cuddle's fur.

"The judges will think this band is brilliant," Chloe said.

"They'll think you're brilliant, too,"

Olivia said. She remembered what Grace had told her about climbing trees. "Why don't you practise reciting the poem to us now? You might feel better."

Chloe sighed. "The Shakespeare poem was my mum's idea. What I really want to do is sing."

"Then that's what you should do!" Grace said. "What's your favourite song?"

"'Cat That Got the Cream'," Chloe replied.

"Sing it for us," Olivia said. "We'd really like you to."

Chloe's cheeks went pink, but she took a deep breath and began.

It was a pop song the girls knew, and they tapped their feet in time. Cuddle swished her tail like a conductor's baton.

Everyone turned to listen. Even The Krazy Katz stopped playing as

Chloe launched into the chorus:

*"Me and my friends, we're a team,*
*We flow together like fish in a stream.*
*We laugh and cry, play and dream,*
*And I feel like the cat that got the cream."*

Everyone broke into applause. "That girl can really sing," said the band's guitarist.

Olivia clapped her hands and Grace put two fingers between her lips, giving a loud whistle.

"Chloe, that was amazing!" Grace said. "You've got to sing for the judges."

"I can't," Chloe said. Her eyes were filling with tears. "I haven't any music

to sing along to. I can't wear this dress.
I don't have my necklace. And –"

Olivia seized Chloe by the shoulders.
"It'll be fine. You've got Grace, Cuddle
and me to help."

Olivia looked Chloe's dress up and
down. "I know just how to make you
the perfect costume. You'll look like a
star! Won't she, Cuddle?"

Cuddle stared up at the three girls.
Then she bolted through the crowd.

Grace shook her head. "Where's that
crazy kitten gone now?"

# Chapter Seven
## Cuddle Makes Some Noise

Grace pushed through the crowd that had gathered. The little kitten bounded towards The Krazy Katz and hopped on to the drummer's lap. He was tall with a ripped T-shirt and a chain hanging round his neck. Grace thought he looked a little scary.

But the drummer's tough face melted into a smile. "Hello, kitty-cat," he said. "Do you want to play?"

Cuddle hopped on to one of the drums, making an echoing *boom*. She flicked her crooked tail in delight, and pounced on the next drum. *Boom!*

Cuddle sprang all over the drum kit, filling the room with noise. *Ba-boom, bang, boom, bang, boooooom!* She finished by swiping the cymbals with her front paw. *Craaaaaaash!*

The girl with pink hair laughed. "I guess she does want to play – play music!"

Grace picked up Cuddle. "I'm so sorry," she began.

But The Krazy Katz were clapping and cheering Cuddle's performance.

"Your kitten should be in our band," the girl with the keyboard said. "She sure is cute."

The pink-haired girl nodded. "Our lead singer has just quit," she said.

"We need a new member."

Grace could feel excitement bubbling inside her like lemonade. "Did you hear my friend Chloe singing?"

They all nodded. "She was brilliant," said the drummer.

"And do you know the song she sang?" Grace asked.

"'Cat That Got The Cream'?" the pink-haired girl asked. "It's my favourite." She strummed the opening notes on her guitar.

Grace beamed and hugged Cuddle. "You need a singer – and Chloe needs a band. Maybe she could sing with you?"

The three Krazy Katz grinned. "That would be fantastic!" the drummer said.

While Grace and Cuddle led the rock band through the busy practice room, Olivia put the finishing touches to Chloe's new outfit. She had used the nail scissors she kept in her sequinned

# Cuddle
## The Magic Kitten

bag to cut the dress diagonally across, so it hung longer on one side than the other, and chopped off the sleeves. She brushed out Chloe's red hair so it swept over her shoulder.

Chloe twirled around on the spot. "Thank you! I feel like a rock star."

"Now all you need is a band," Grace said with a smile. "Chloe, these are The Krazy Katz."

"Hi, Chloe," the girl with pink hair said. "We'd love you to sing with us."

"I'd like that!" Chloe replied.

Cuddle twitched her whiskers. Sparkly blue star brooches appeared on Chloe and the two Krazy Katz girls, and a glittery blue baseball cap appeared on the drummer's head. They matched Cuddle's shining eyes.

"Where did these come from?" Chloe exclaimed, stroking the twinkling jewels in her brooch.

"Cuddle can do more than play the drums," Olivia said, scratching Cuddle behind her black-tipped ear. "She's a magic kitten!"

"Maybe Cuddle should be in the show," the girl with the pink hair said. "She's definitely got talent!"

The door to the practice room opened and the stage manager stuck his head round. "Chloe!" he called. "It's your turn to perform."

Grace squeezed Chloe's hand.

"Come on, it's time to go."

But Chloe shook her head. "I can't do it," she said.

"There's nothing to worry about," Olivia replied, putting an arm around her. "You've got a new outfit, a band – and an amazing voice."

"There's one thing I haven't got," Chloe said, looking at the floor. "My good luck charm."

"You don't need luck," Grace said. "You've got talent."

Chloe looked up. "Really?"

Olivia nodded. "And you've got me, Grace and Cuddle to cheer you on. Friends are the best lucky charm of all!"

# Chapter Eight
## A Starry Success

Olivia, Grace and Cuddle watched as Chloe and The Krazy Katz performed onstage. The crowd was clapping along to the beat.

"Looks like my daughter doesn't need this any more," a voice behind them said. It was Chloe's mum, smiling.

She slid Chloe's lucky necklace into her handbag.

Cuddle bounded across the stage and leapt on to the drummer's lap. "Look, Cuddle wants to be a rock star, too," Grace said.

The pink-haired girl swung her guitar as she played, and Cuddle tapped the cymbals with her paw. *Swish, swish. Boom-boom-swish.*

Then Chloe started to sing. Olivia and Grace peeked out behind the curtains.

The judges were swaying along, and Tony was using his pen to tap out a rhythm on the table.

"She looks so happy," Chloe's mum

# Cuddle
The Magic Kitten

said. "Thank you for helping her."

"That's OK," Grace replied. "It was fun."

The song ended with a long high note from Chloe, and a huge *craaaash* as Cuddle used both of her front paws to swipe the cymbals. The audience leapt to its feet, cheering and clapping as Chloe confidently strode to the front of the stage and gave them a deep curtsy.

"Bravo!" yelled the young magician, tossing his top hat into the air.

Tony held up his hand and the cheers faded away. Grace linked her arm nervously through Olivia's.

What would the judges say?

Tony's face was serious. He leant forward in his seat. "Chloe," he said, "do you know how that song made me feel?"

TONY

Chloe shook her head.

"Then I'll tell you," Tony said. The girls held their breath, but he suddenly grinned. "Like the cat that got the cream. I loved it!"

The audience erupted into applause. "Go, Chloe!" Olivia shouted, as the girls whirled each other round.

Tony's white teeth gleamed. "Congratulations, Chloe. You and The Krazy Katz are stars!"

Chloe ran offstage where her mum caught her in a hug.

"Well done," Grace said, patting Chloe on the back. "You deserve it!"

"It's all thanks to you," Chloe replied, "and Cuddle."

The little kitten pushed into the middle of the three girls. She bumped her furry head against Chloe's ankles, then weaved through Grace and Olivia's feet.

They could feel her purr rumbling through them.

"It's time for us to go," Grace said. "Goodbye, Chloe!"

"Goodbye!" Olivia called.

Chloe and the Star Maker stage became a whirling blur of colour, and the girls shut their eyes.

\*\*\*

When Grace opened her eyes again, she and Olivia were lying on the springy grass in Olivia's garden.

"That was so much fun," Grace said,

giving a delighted wriggle. "Wasn't Chloe brave?"

"She was," Olivia agreed. "And now it's my turn to be brave. I'm going to climb the cherry tree!"

The two girls ran to the trunk. Grace swung on to the lowest branch then stretched out her hand.

Olivia grabbed it and Grace helped her scramble up.

"You're climbing the tree!" Grace cried.

*Jingle jangle jingle.*

Cuddle was sitting on the branch above them, surrounded by pompoms of blossom. She held out a front paw as if she was waving goodbye, then disappeared in a haze of sparkles.

"Goodbye, Cuddle," the girls called.
"See you soon!"

# Cuddle
### The Magic Kitten

Olivia tucked a blossom behind her ear. "Do you know how sitting up here makes me feel?" she asked.

**Cuddle**
The Magic Kitten

Grace laughed, and both girls cried,
"Like the cat that got the cream!"

# Cuddle
## The Magic Kitten

Can't wait to find out
what Cuddle will do next?
Then read on! Here is the first
chapter from Cuddle's third
story, Princess Party Sleepover ...

# Cuddle
## The Magic Kitten

## PRINCESS PARTY SLEEPOVER
### Hayley Daze

# Cuddle
## The Magic Kitten

# PRINCESS PARTY SLEEPOVER

It was a warm summer's evening and Olivia's bedroom window was wide open. Purple wisteria flowers nodded against the sill. Furry bumblebees buzzed from flower to flower, collecting the last of the day's pollen. The setting sun made the tower blocks and houses of Catterton glow a rosy pink.

"Our first sleepover!" Olivia squealed, twirling in her pink, ruffled nightie.

"I've never been to a sleepover before," Grace said, doing up the last button of her favourite star-patterned

pyjamas.

"Me neither," Olivia said. "What should we do first?" The girls flopped on Olivia's bed, which had a fluffy pink duvet.

"Let's play princesses," Olivia suggested. She leapt to her feet,

wobbling on her bed. She wrapped her
duvet around her shoulders like a royal
robe. "Ta-dah!" she said and pretended
to wave at her loyal subjects.

"Hello, princess!" Grace said and
bowed to Olivia.

"Now it's your turn," Olivia said,
jumping down to sit beside Grace.
"You'd make a lovely princess."

Grace shook her head, making her
blonde ponytail fly about. "No way!
Who wants to be a princess and have to
wear dresses and go to boring parties?
Yuck!"

Olivia stared open-mouthed at her
friend. "I would love to be a princess,
trying on all those lovely outfits and

tiaras."

Suddenly, the setting sun sent a golden beam of light directly through the open window.

"Maybe Cuddle's coming!" Olivia said, looking down into her back garden.

The girls couldn't wait to see the magical kitten again. Cuddle always arrived in a burst of sunshine and took them on amazing adventures.

Just then, a sound drifted through the window.

*Jingle jangle jingle.*

"That's her bell!" Grace cried. The wisteria branch beneath Olivia's window was shaking, its flowers bobbing up and down. A tiny white tail flicked out from the quivering leaves, a

kink in its black tip.

"Cuddle!" both girls shouted.

The kitten's blue eyes flashed as she scrambled onto the windowsill, the silver bell on her pink collar jangling. She sprang between the girls into Olivia's room, landing in the middle of the bed. "Miaow!"

Cuddle bounced onto Olivia's shoulder. She scooped the kitten up, cradling her upside-down to show her tummy.

"Cuddle's purring," Olivia said, her eyes shining. "That means we're going on another adventure!"

"Where are you going to take us, Cuddle?" Grace asked, nuzzling Cuddle nose-to-nose.

Cuddle's purr grew louder and louder, buzzing like the bumblebees outside. The girls' skin tingled all over, making them giggle. Grace and Olivia squeezed their eyes tightly shut.

"Here we go!" Olivia said.

***

## To be continued ...